MW00533041

Chowder

Chowder FOR BREAKFAST, AND *chowder* FOR DINNER, AND *chowder* FOR SUPPER, TILL YOU BEGAN TO LOOK FOR *fish-bones* COMING THROUGH YOUR CLOTHES.

Herman Melville

Chowder

AMERICAN ROOTS

Applewood Books
CARLISLE, MASSACHUSETTS

The short works Applewood includes in its American Roots series have been selected to connect us. The books are tactile mementos of American passions by some of America's most famous writers. Each of these has meant something very personal to me.

Reading *Chowder* set me off onto a journey of discovery: whaling, ships, life at sea, clams, cod, salt, whale oil, sea chanties and other music, colors, people's livelihoods and wealth, nineteenth-century literature, and more. For months I was thinking only of chowder-related things. When I shared this with two very close friends, whom I hoped would break me of this obsession, they let me in on their secret: they fell in love over *Moby Dick*.

> "*Chowder for breakfast, and chowder for dinner, and chowder for supper, till you began to look for fish-bones coming through your clothes.*"

⟋Phil Zuckerman
PUBLISHER

It was quite late in the evening when the little Moss came snugly to anchor, and Queequeg and I went ashore; so we could attend to no business that day, at least none but a supper and a bed. The landlord of the Spouter-Inn had recommended us to his cousin Hosea Hussey of the Try Pots, whom he asserted to be the proprietor of one of the best kept hotels in all Nantucket, and moreover he had assured us that Cousin Hosea, as he called him, was famous for his chowders. In short, he plainly hinted that we could not possibly do better than try pot-luck at the Try Pots. But the directions he had given us about keeping a yellow ware-house on our starboard hand till we opened a white church to the larboard, and then keeping that on the larboard hand till we made a corner three points to the starboard, and that done, then ask the first man we met where the place was; these crooked directions of his very much puzzled us at first, especially as, at the outset, Quequeg insisted that the yellow warehouse—our first

2

point of departure—must be left on the larboard hand, whereas I had understood Peter Coffin to say it was on the starboard. However, by dint of beating about a little in the dark, and now and then knocking up a peaceful inhabitant to inquire the way, we at last came to something which there was no mistaking.

Two enormous wooden pots painted black, and suspended by asses' ears, swung from the cross-trees of an old top-mast, planted in front of an old doorway. The horns of the cross-trees were sawed off on the other side, so that this old top-mast looked

3

not a little like a gallows. Perhaps I was over sensitive to such impressions at the time, but I could not help staring at this gallows with a vague misgiving. A sort of crick was in my neck as I gazed up to the two remaining horns; yes, two of them, one for Queequeg, and one for me. It's ominous, thinks I. A Coffin my Innkeeper upon landing in my first whaling port; tombstones staring at me in the whalemen's chapel, and here a gallows! and a pair of prodigious black pots too! Are these last throwing out oblique hints touching Tophet?

4   I was called from these reflections

by the sight of a freckled woman
with yellow hair and a yellow
gown, standing in the porch of
the inn, under a dull red lamp
swinging there, that looked much
like an injured eye, and carrying
on a brisk scolding with a man in
a purple woollen shirt.

"Get along with ye," said she to
the man, "or I'll be combing ye!"

"Come on, Queequeg," said I,
"all right. There's Mrs. Hussey."

And so it turned out; Mr.
Hosea Hussey being from home,
but leaving Mrs. Hussey entirely
competent to attend to all his
affairs. Upon making known our
desires for a supper and a bed,   5

Mrs. Hussey, postponing further scolding for the present, ushered us into a little room, and seating us at a table spread with the relics of a recently concluded repast, turned round to us and said—"Clam or Cod?"

"What's that about Cods, ma'am?" said I, with much politeness.

"Clam or Cod?" she repeated.

"A clam for supper? a cold clam; is that what you mean, Mrs. Hussey?" says I, "but that's a rather cold and clammy reception in the winter time, ain't it, Mrs. Hussey?"

But being in a great hurry to resume scolding the man in the purple shirt who was waiting for it in the entry, and seeming to hear nothing but the word "clam," Mrs. Hussey hurried towards an open door leading to the kitchen, and bawling out "clam for two," disappeared.

"Queequeg," said I, "do you think that we can make a supper for us both on one clam?"

However, a warm savory steam from the kitchen served to belie the apparently cheerless prospect before us. But when that smoking chowder came in, the mystery was delightfully explained. Oh! sweet friends, hearken to me. It was made of small juicy clams, scarcely bigger than hazel nuts, mixed with pounded ship biscuits, and salted pork cut up into little flakes! the whole enriched with butter, and plentifully seasoned with pepper and salt. Our appetites being sharpened by the frosty voyage, and in particular, Queequeg seeing his favourite fishing food before him, and the chowder being surpassingly excellent, we despatched it with great expedition: when leaning back a moment and bethinking me of Mrs. Hussey's clam and cod announcement, I thought I would try a little experiment. Stepping to the kitchen door, I uttered the word

8

"cod" with great emphasis, and resumed my seat. In a few moments the savoury steam came forth again, but with a different flavor, and in good time a fine cod-chowder was placed before us.

We resumed business; and while plying our spoons in the bowl, thinks I to myself, I wonder now if this here has any effect on the head? What's that stultifying saying about chowder-headed people? "But look, Queequeg, ain't that a live eel in your bowl? Where's your harpoon?"

Fishiest of all fishy places was the Try Pots, which well 9

deserved its name; for the pots there were always boiling chowders. Chowder for breakfast, and chowder for dinner, and chowder for supper, till you began to look for fish-bones coming through your clothes. The area before the house was paved with clam-shells. Mrs. Hussey wore a polished necklace of codfish vertebra; and Hosea Hussey had his account books bound in superior old shark-skin. There was a fishy flavor to the milk, too, which I could not at all account for, till one morning happening to take a stroll along the beach among some fishermen's boats, I saw Hosea's brindled cow feeding on fish remnants, and marching along the sand with each foot in a cod's decapitated head, looking very slipshod, I assure ye.

Supper concluded, we received a lamp, and directions from Mrs. Hussey concerning the nearest way to bed; but, as Queequeg was about to precede me up the stairs, the lady reached forth her arm, and demanded his harpoon; she allowed no harpoon in her chambers. "Why not? said I; "every true whaleman sleeps with his harpoon—but why not?" "Because it's dangerous," says she. "Ever since young Stiggs coming from that unfort'nt v'y'ge of his, when he was gone four years and a half, with only three barrels of ile, was found dead in my first floor back, with his harpoon in his side; ever since then I allow no boarders to take sich dangerous weepons in their rooms at night. So, Mr. Queequeg" (for she had learned his name), "I will just take this here iron, and keep it for you till morning. But the chowder; clam or cod to-morrow for breakfast, men?"

"Both," says I; "and let's have a couple of smoked herring by way of variety."